The Screaming House

D.L. WINCHESTER

Undertaker Books

Undertaker Books
www.undertakerbooks.com

Cover Design: Dakota Marquart

First edition 2024

The Screaming House

For Wednesday.

CHAPTER 1
TIDWELL

J ohn Tidwell lay on the cot, tears flowing as he held the blood-covered dress against his chest.

Having his balls crushed in pliers hadn't hurt like this.

Neither had having his knee smashed with a sledgehammer, or having every joint in his arms and legs pulled out of place.

Some things had been painful enough to send him into unconsciousness, but the escape was temporary, and the tortures resumed when he awakened.

Now, the torture was done, but he still hurt.

Ray Spencer had smiled when he told him what he did to Millie, the woman Tidwell loved.

Tidwell had tried to reach through the bars, to grab the son-of-a-bitch and mete out some torture of his own. Spencer had stepped back and laughed at him, before throwing the dress into his cell.

"Something to remember her by," he called as he left the room.

Tidwell wondered if it was a trick, a psychological torture meant to break him further.

No.

He'd heard the screams from the next room.

"If you don't be quiet," a voice mumbled from the bed outside the cell, "I'll come in there and give you something to cry about."

The Doctor.

The miserable asshole keeping Tidwell alive so Spencer could keep torturing him.

He knew he shouldn't have skimmed money from Spencer's accounts, but the temptation had been too great. Spencer had more money than anyone needed; what was a few thousand to him?

Now Tidwell would never have a chance to spend his ill-gotten gains, would never be able to escape with Millie and build the life they dreamed of together.

As he stared at the ceiling, tears still silently falling, he wondered why he didn't give up, surrender to the pain and punishment meted out by Spencer and the Doctor.

Closing his eyes, he saw Millie's face and knew.

He wasn't going down without a fight.

CHAPTER 2

ROCHE

"I'll bet twenty." The gray-eyed cowboy across the table tossed a double eagle into the pot.

Jack Roche studied the mural behind his opponent. The painter had talent, even if his taste was questionable. Every detail of his subject, a nude, full-figured blonde, was present to be admired. Roche wondered if she was Delilah, the namesake of the saloon, or another woman who'd passed through this god-forsaken town.

"It's your bet," the dealer said, snapping Roche out of his thoughts.

Running his finger along the edge of the card, he felt where the edges had been shaved down, marking the cards to allow a skilled dealer to manipulate the deck. But he wasn't ready to let these two know he had caught on to their crooked game.

Picking up his cards, he looked over the top of them at the cowboy. He was leaning back in his chair, cards face down on the table. A toothpick appeared in his hand, and he twirled it between his fingers, a relaxed grin on his face.

"Are you going to play, Roche?" the dealer pushed. He was another cowboy, younger than the other, with sandy blonde hair and shit-brown eyes.

"I'm thinking," Roche replied.

He had reason to think. These two had taken him for almost a thousand dollars in the last four hours as he waited for an opportunity to present itself. Seeing the marked card Roche introduced the last time he dealt in the gray-eyed cowboy's hand along with a card Roche marked with a bent corner, he realized the moment was nigh.

He picked up a double eagle off the green felt table and tossed it into the pot. "I'll call."

Next to him, the snake-oil salesman tossed his cards on the table. "Fold. Too rich for me."

The dealer glanced at his cards, then tossed a pair of double eagles into the pot. "Raise."

Fuck, these boys were greedy. A double eagle, $20, was almost as much as most men made in a month. There would be nine on the table if Gray Eyes and Roche called the raise, in addition to assorted small bills and coins.

Combined, the pot was more than most men made in a year.

The high-stakes game had drawn a crowd, even as it stretched into the early morning.

Gray Eyes tossed another double eagle onto the table. "Call the raise."

Roche snuck a glance at the mirror that covered the mural's sex. It showed a closed door on the balcony, one he wanted to see cracked open before he made his move.

Reaching in his pocket, Roche pulled out a handful of bills. Counting out twenty dollars, he tossed it in the pot. "Luck's got to turn soon."

"That's the spirit," Gray Eyes said with a smile.

"Wish I could raise again," the dealer said, looking down at his hand. "But I guess that's enough. Show 'em, friends."

Gray Eyes laid down his cards. "Full house, sixes over queens."

On the balcony, a door banged open, distracting the crowd. Roche discreetly checked the mirror and smiled. His door was cracked, a single eye looking out over a pistol barrel.

"That's awfully interesting," Roche said, laying down his cards. "I've also got a full house, queens over nines."

The room went silent as the crowd stared at the five queens on the tabletop.

"You cheating bastards!" The snake-oil salesman jumped to his feet.

"Takes one to know one!" Gray Eyes shot back. "The shit you sell heal gunshot wounds?"

A slow shake of the man's head.

"Then sit your ass down while we sort this out!"

"Ain't much to sort out here, the five queens speak for themselves," Roche said. "But I reckon we need to talk about that bank robbery in Clairesville."

"Clairesville?" the dealer asked.

"Shut up, Earl," Gray Eyes said.

Reaching in his pocket, Roche took out a pair of wanted posters, unfolded them, and tossed them on top of the pot.

"Them drawings look like you, except you're uglier in person," Roche said.

The dealer and Gray Eyes looked down at the posters, then up at Roche. "You the law?" the dealer asked.

"Law enough."

"Bounty hunter?" Gray eyes asked.

A nod. "Them posters say you're worth a thousand each, dead or alive. I aim to collect that, plus the money you've swindled out of me tonight."

The cowboy laughed. "Mister, you can't just roll into our hometown and expect to put one over on us. No one here's gonna let you haul us off to Clairesville, no matter what we've done."

Roche tapped the poster. "Dead or alive, boys. I don't figure there'll be a lot of fight over your rotting carcasses."

"You can't plug us both before one of us gets you," the dealer challenged, slamming his fists on the table.

Roche realized the distraction as he saw a flash of metal appear above the table. Ignoring it, he went for the gun in his shoulder holster as a gunshot sounded from the balcony.

Revolver in hand, Roche aimed across the table and fired as the dealer's gun came up. The man's eyes went wide as his heart tried to beat in spite of the lead slug that had pierced it. His gun fell to the floor, and he slumped back in his chair as Roche turned to look at Gray Eyes.

He was dead, a channel carved into the top of his skull to reveal blood and brains.

Roche glanced at the mirror to see the door on the balcony had closed. Good.

Reaching onto the table, he began to rake in the pot.

"The hell do you think you're doing?" someone called from the crowd.

"He done killed the Spencers!" another voice called. Roche breathed a sigh of relief. It seemed his associate on the balcony had gone unnoticed.

"Hang the sidewinder!"

Forgetting the money, Roche climbed onto the table, a second revolver appearing in his hand. "Friends, I may be in hell before the night's over, but if you're inclined to try anything foolish, I'll punch your ticket before I go."

"He's bluffing!" a big man in the front row yelled. "Let's settle his hash!"

Roche fired, drilling him through the eye before he could take a step.

"Line's gettin' longer, folks."

Slowly, the crowd began to slip away, until all that remained was an ugly man in a battered hat. He spit a stream of tobacco juice onto the floor, then looked up at Roche. "Reckon when Judge Spencer finds out what you've done, you ain't gonna be so tough."

"I'll cross that bridge when I get to it."

The batwings at the front of the saloon banged open, and a fat, bald man with a gold badge pinned to his shirt came in. His narrow eyes studied the room, settling on the three bodies around the table.

"What the hell happened here?"

Roche used his revolver to gesture at the bodies. "Had a disagreement over cards."

"Looks like more than a disagreement." He stepped closer, then froze. "Jesus, them's the Spencers!"

"That's what it says on these wanted posters." Roche hopped to the floor and holstered one of his pistols before picking up the papers. "You'll note they say 'Dead or Alive.'"

The crowd was returning, emboldened by the sheriff's presence.

"Git 'im, Sheriff," someone called.

"No need to try the snake, let's string his ass up!"

The sheriff pulled his pistol and fired it into the air, bringing a shower of plaster down from the ceiling.

"Hey!" the bartender yelled. "I don't want no skylight!"

The sheriff's gun lowered, aimed between the man's eyes. "How 'bout a hole in your head?"

The bartender paused, staring into the gun's mouth before slowly shaking his head.

"Didn't figure." He lowered the gun and turned to the mob. "Now as for the rest of you, he'll get what's coming to him, but we're gonna do it nice and legal." A shit-eating grin crossed his face as he faced Roche. "Tomorrow, you'll go before Judge Spencer, and the next day, I'll hang your ass. Now drop that gun."

Roche leveled it at the sheriff. "Not happening, Sheriff. This was justified, and I got the wanted posters even if it wasn't."

"Ain't nothing justified in this town unless I say it is!" the sheriff snarled. "Wanted posters mean jack shit around here. Way I see it, you done killed a pair of upstanding citizens."

"If they're upstanding citizens, I'd hate to see your low-lifes."

A floorboard next to Roche creaked, and he turned his head in time to see a gun barrel descend, knocking him unconscious.

CHAPTER 3

AGGIE

No one had noticed.

Aggie walked down the stairs as the sheriff hauled Roche away. A couple of the crowd glanced at her, the peek-a-boo gown pushing up her cleavage.

But they didn't realize she'd been involved in the shooting.

She could have killed the sheriff, or shot the deputy who snuck up on Roche, but that would have incited the mob, and lowered their odds of escape. Better to wait and spring Roche from the jail outside town.

He was still "Roche" to her, not "Papa," even after riding with him for two years.

At the poker table, the snake oil salesman was busy shoveling money into his pockets. He'd be out of town before daybreak, Aggie guessed, never to return to Briar City.

She felt a hand on her ass, and turned to find a cowboy stepping back to size her up.

"All that action gets a man's dander up," he said, smiling. "You want some business?"

She smiled and took his hand. "I'll show you a good time, cowboy."

Aggie had been in town a week already, working in the saloon and watching the Spencer brothers prance through town like they were kings. Two of them, at least. She'd heard rumors of a third brother, older and meaner, who ran Briar City and his brothers with an iron fist.

She'd told Roche, but he just shook his head.

"Ray Spencer ain't on any wanted poster. Let's get the two we came to get and mosey on up the trail."

They'd gotten the two, but now Roche was in jail, and Ray would get the news soon enough.

As she led the cowboy into her room, Aggie couldn't help but wonder how Ray Spencer would feel about them moseying on up the trail.

CHAPTER 4

ROCHE

Roche's head hurt.

He opened his eyes to see wooden rafters above him. Slowly, he wiggled his fingers, then his toes.

At least everything seemed to be working, even with a cracked noggin.

Slowly, the events of the night before came back to him: the Spencers, the crowd, the sheriff, the sneak that conked him.

Why hadn't he just shot him?

He inhaled, and almost gagged. The bed he was on stank of piss and vomit, and the tattered quilt thrown over him wasn't much better.

Roche turned his head, looking across the cell at the log wall. It looked plenty thick. He wasn't gonna get out by cutting through it, that was for sure.

There wasn't even a window to squeeze through.

Someone cleared their throat, and Roche sat up to see a man standing outside the cell.

He looked like someone had combined the two gamblers he'd shot the night before. His gray eyes pierced Roche, his graying blonde hair pulled back in a ponytail under a gray Stetson.

"So you're the son-of-a-bitch who killed James and Earl?"

"Don't know about that." Roche swung his legs off the bed. God, his head hurt. Whoever cracked him hadn't held back.

"You're saying you didn't kill them?"

"No, I'm saying I ain't a son-of-a-bitch."

Roche looked over and saw the man's face growing red. "I don't give a damn what you think! You killed my brothers!"

"I killed a couple of bank robbers. Didn't much care who they were related to." Roche got to his feet, and had to reach out for the wall to steady himself. "Kinda like they didn't care about the families of the bank manager and his clerk."

"Who the fuck are you to judge?" the man demanded.

Roche shrugged. "Ain't no one, just trying to earn an honest living."

Now he laughed. "That's rich. But you ain't gonna be livin' much longer."

Roche nodded at the revolver on the man's hip. "You gonna play 'fish in a barrel?'"

A shake of the head. "Naw. That'd be too damn quick for my tastes." He turned to someone standing out of sight. "Hang this son-of-a-bitch, Sheriff!"

Roche stepped toward the bars. "I done told you, the shooting was justified."

A grin crept across the man's face. "Don't much give a damn what you think. I'm the judge, and you're the condemned." He spit tobacco juice in Roche's face. "Court is adjourned."

CHAPTER 5

TIDWELL

Tidwell didn't know how long it had been since the torture had ended.

Sometimes it felt like he slept for days as his body struggled to recover from what the Doctor and Ray had done to it.

Other times, pain kept him awake through the night, twisting and tensing to avoid crying out and wakening the Doctor.

But he was healing, slowly.

With the help of a cane, he could hobble from his bed to the bucket in the corner that served as his toilet.

Sitting up, he reached for his cane to make another trip.

Across the room, the Doctor was sitting on his bed, watching. The Doctor smiled as Tidwell hobbled across his cell and sat on the bucket.

Tidwell was embarrassed, sitting there with no way to control the trickle flowing between his legs.

"You'll be ready for the next stage soon," the Doctor said, getting to his feet and walking to the door.

As Tidwell watched the Doctor go, he wondered what the next stage would be.

Spencer had told him it would be worse than anything that had already been done to him.

Tidwell didn't know how that was possible.

But he believed it.

Chapter 6

ROCHE

Roche woke from a nap to the sound of hammering outside the jail.

"What the fuck is that," he muttered, putting a hand to his head. The banging was amplifying the pain, making it dance around his skull.

"They're getting ready for tomorrow," a voice said from the cell door, and Roche looked up to find Ray Spencer standing there. "Putting the gallows together."

"I figured you'd be more excited." How long had he been standing like that, staring down at Roche while he slept?

"I figured you'd protest more."

Roche shrugged. "I can tell when the railroad's comin' through. All yellin' and fussin' would do is make my headache worse."

A grin crept across Spencer's face. Stepping away from the cell, he returned with a hammer and started banging it on the bars.

"How's this?"

Roche covered his ears and dove onto the bed, burying his head under the pillow. Behind him, he heard the cell door open, then the blanket and pillow were pulled away.

"You miserable jackass," Spencer hissed, his rotten breath standing out against the stink of the mattress. "I wish I could give you what you really deserve."

Roche slammed his elbow into Spencer's jaw, knocking him away. Sitting up, he shook his head to try to clear the pain.

Spencer's punch drove him back, busting his nose and causing blood to cascade down Roche's face. Falling back, he managed to keep his head from hitting the wall, but the pain of the blow made his head hurt more.

"You like this torture shit, don't you?"

Spencer laughed. "This here is just a taste."

Roche sat up, holding his head in his hands to steady it. "Looks like the whole damn family is rotten."

Spencer raised his fist, and Roche put up a hand to block it, drawing laughter.

"I don't want to knock you out," Spencer said, lowering his arm. "I want you to spend your last twenty-four hours thinking about what's coming. There's quick ways to hang a man, and there's slow ways. You're gonna die slow, the rope digging into your neck as you kick and squirm. I hope you're conscious 'til the end, feeling your body try to save itself from the icy hand of death. It won't work though, and my brothers will be waiting for you at the gates of hell."

"Seems awful brutal for a man just doing his job," Roche said.

Spencer grabbed the front of his shirt and lifted him off the bunk. "You killed my brothers for a measly thousand bucks."

"No," Roche said.

"No?"

"A thousand each. That makes two for the both."

Spencer dropped him, letting Roche fall to the floor. "I'll have a check for you in the morning. We'll see if you can spend it where you're headed." Spitting a glob of tobacco onto Roche, he stomped out of the cell, slamming the door behind him.

CHAPTER 7
AGGIE

Sitting alone in her room, Aggie watched the sun descend in the sky as she prepared for a busy night. A group of cowboys had just hit town, payroll in hand, and the saloon would be busy.

Perfect for what Aggie had planned.

A commotion always helped a jailbreak.

Pulling on her gown, Aggie thought about the man she'd be rescuing tonight.

She was seventeen when she finally met her father.

Roche had been stationed at Fort Davis, in Texas's Big Bend country. Her mother, Ysidra, had worked at the Fort with her father as a civilian cleaner. She and Roche fell in love on the banks of Limpia Creek, but when Ysidra's father found out, he was furious. Roche returned from a patrol to learn his beloved had been taken back to Mexico.

Shortly after, the Civil War broke out, and Roche left Fort Davis to serve in the Union Army.

When Ysidra learned she was pregnant, her father returned to the fort looking for Roche, but he had already left. Returning to Ojinaga, Aggie's *abuelo* had christened her "Magdalena" shortly after she was born.

"She'll probably be a whore like her mother," he'd said, holding his granddaughter in his arms. "But with the Lord, there is always hope."

Before long, "Magdalena" was shortened to "Aggie" by Ysidra, who never liked the name her father had chosen.

Raised in Mexico, Aggie had been looked down on by her *abuelo* as a bastard. Even worse, her blue eyes and pale skin made her stand out among the other children, and she was constantly teased about her looks.

Until she learned to shoot.

Stealing her *abuelo*'s rifle when he left to deliver supplies to the mine at Shafter, she'd go out into the desert with the rifle in one hand and a bag of empty whiskey bottles in the other; she practiced until her shoulder ached from the repeated recoil. Staggering back to town, she returned the rifle to its spot, then went to the well for water, walking lopsided through the streets and drawing more laughter.

Then, one day, she was sitting on the porch when she heard a scream from the house across the street.

"El crotalo!"

Grabbing the rifle, she ran to find a terrified mother on the porch, her two-year-old in the dusty yard.

And five feet away, the coiled rattlesnake, waiting to strike.

Aggie didn't hesitate. She raised the rifle and fired, blowing the snake's head off.

The child looked at her, then ran screaming to its mother.

After that, even if the other children didn't like Aggie, they at least respected her. Which made the beating she took from her *abuelo* when he found out she'd been using his rifle almost worth it.

Her mother never stopped looking north, hoping to see a lone rider coming down the road from Fort Davis. For a while, Aggie looked too, but as she got older, her hope of meeting her father faded.

Finally, at sixteen, Aggie had enough of her *abuelo*'s abuse. It was bad enough the way he taunted her mother about Roche leaving her, but he also insisted Roche had abandoned them forever.

Aggie decided to prove the old asshole wrong.

Stealing his horse and rifle, she set out in search of Roche. Tracking him to Fort Dodge in Kansas, she learned he had left the army a month before in pursuit of a pair of ex-soldiers who had robbed a bank.

Six months later, she caught up to the soldiers outside the Hole-In-The-Wall hideout in Wyoming. They bragged about leaving Roche to die in a nearby canyon, and tried to rape Aggie. She gunned them down with the Smith and Wesson now hidden under her bed.

Finding Roche, she managed to get him to a nearby army post, where a friend of his convinced the surgeon to treat him. Aggie'd stayed by his side during his recovery, getting to know her father.

"Why did you never come back?" she'd asked one day, walking across the parade ground with him.

He looked up and sighed. "Your grandfather sent me a letter after the war. Well, not to me, since he didn't know where I was, but to the War Department, asking them to forward it to me. He said your mother had married and there was no room for me in her life." A shrug. "He didn't even mention I had a daughter."

Aggie's face had burned red. "That's lies, all lies."

Roche shrugged. "How was I to know? I didn't want to hurt you all, so I decided to move on."

If her *abuelo* had been standing there, Aggie would have killed him. Instead, she threw her arms around her father's neck.

"There will always be room for you in my life," she whispered.

When the time came to ride on, she'd accepted his offer to go with him, and they'd formed their bounty hunting partnership.

CHAPTER 8

ROCHE

"You got off easy," the deputy said as he passed Roche a bowl of stew.

"The hell you say." Roche felt the knot on his skull. It was still painful, but getting better. At least the hammering outside was done, even if the cell was getting darker. "You the one who gave me this?"

A nod. "Slipped in the back while you were talkin' to the sheriff."

"Did you have to hit me so hard?"

Laughter. "Didn't want you gettin' up, the way you work with those guns."

"I can understand that." Roche sat on the bed, holding the bowl in his lap. The soup was cold, but at least it was food. "What do you mean, I got off easy."

"Even a slow hangin' is better than what Ray Spencer does out at the Screaming House."

"The Screaming House?" Roche put the bowl to his lips and slurped. It wasn't bad, just cold.

"He's got a place out on his spread, 'bout half a day's ride from the main house. Some kind of old logging camp he converted into a torture chamber."

Roche took another slurp. "That don't seem too legal."

A laugh. "'Round here, the law is what Ray Spencer says it is. If a whore or wanderer disappears every once in a while, we don't say nothin'. Healthier that way, you know?"

"I can understand that."

"Reckon he'll be haulin' someone else out there soon, blowing off some steam after what you did to his brothers." The deputy shuddered. "If I knew I was headed to the Screaming House, I'd put a bullet through my head. The things I've heard, what he does out there, they ain't right."

Finishing the soup, Roche handed the bowl back through the bars. "So why let him do it?"

The deputy shrugged. "He ain't doin' them to me. It's easier to just pretend it don't happen than to invite trouble by stirring up a fuss."

CHAPTER 9

AGGIE

A ggie untied her corset and stuffed it into one of the saddle bags, on top of the low-cut dress she'd been wearing. Hopefully, she wouldn't need it again for a while.

Stepping in front of the mirror, she studied her lean body. Aggie's skin was tan, the combination of a white father and a Hispanic mother. Her dark hair and features reflected her mother, but the piercing blue eyes were all Roche.

She let her eyes wander, admiring her curves. Aggie had changed a lot since she left her home in Ojinaga, but her body had changed the most. No longer the skinny, flat body of a girl, she was becoming a woman. Except her breasts, damn it. She didn't even have to bind her chest, they were so small.

Downstairs, someone yelled, breaking her chain of thought.

Enough vanity. There was work to do.

She grabbed the pants off the bed and pulled them on before taking a blue shirt from the back of a chair. Buttoning it, she stuffed the tail into the pants before positioning her suspenders.

Her shoulder-length black hair was quickly swept into a bun and hidden under her gray hat. At first glance, Aggie looked like a man.

As half of a bounty hunting partnership, that's exactly how she wanted to look.

Tonight, no one would recognize her as the working girl who'd drifted into town a week earlier.

Strapping on her gun belt, she checked to make sure her revolver was loaded. A Smith and Wesson Model 3, she'd carried it since before she caught up to Roche, two years before. Roche said it was a woman's gun; Aggie said it was all the gun she needed.

In the small of her back, behind her belt, she concealed a two-shot derringer, a habit she'd picked up from Roche.

"It never hurts to have an ace up your sleeve," he'd told her.

Taking the saddlebags from the bed, she stepped out onto the balcony and looked down at the table in the corner. A poker game was in progress, the hole from her bullet still visible in the wall behind the players.

Life goes on.

She slipped down the back stairs and out of the saloon.

CHAPTER 10
TIDWELL

T idwell leaned on the cane as he walked across the wooden floor of his cell. Any misstep would send bolts of pain shooting from his feet through his knees, past his hips and straight to his heart.

It felt like he imagined being struck by lightning must feel, the pain surging through his body with no regard for him at all.

Inwardly, he cursed Spencer and the Doctor for what they had done to him.

Cursing them out loud had cost him his tongue.

Making it to his bed, he lay down and stared up at the ceiling, imagining what he would do when he was free.

He'd start with Spencer, he decided. The Doctor would watch as Tidwell killed Spencer quickly, brutally. Maybe he'd hoist Spencer by the ankles and slit his throat, letting the blood cascade down his face as he screamed his last.

The Doctor would breathe a sigh of relief, expecting the revenge to be short and sweet.

But it wouldn't be. Not for the Doctor.

Not for the architect of the torture Spencer loved and needed.

For him, death would come slowly.

He imagined having a thousand long needles and plunging each of them into a different, non-lethal part of the Doctor's flesh. Finally, when the pain was almost too much for the Doctor to bear, he'd slice the man's guts open and let him fall to the ground, struggling to contain his innards as Tidwell watched his life slowly slip away.

That's what the Doctor deserved.

CHAPTER 11
AGGIE

The sheriff's office was located on the far end of town, away from the main street and its businesses. Aggie crept around the back of the building, peeking in a window.

Deputy Perkins was leaned back in the desk chair, fast asleep. She liked Perkins; he'd been in her bed twice since she'd arrived in town, and told her a lot about the sheriff's office and how things worked.

Men liked to talk after sex, especially when their partner was as attentive as Aggie.

Too bad he had to die.

Pulling her gun, she crept across the porch and eased open the door.

A bell jingled, and Perkins woke with a start.

"What?"

A flash, and a dark hole appeared on Perkins' white shirt, blood flowing as he slumped back into the chair.

"Jesus, couldn't you have slit his throat?"

She looked over at Roche, sitting on the bed and holding his head. "Headache?"

"Your friend there whacked me over the head last night."

Aggie grinned. "Don't worry. He won't do it again."

Snatching the keys from their hook, Aggie walked to the cell and unlocked it.

"Hold it right there!"

Aggie turned to see the sheriff standing in the doorway, his gun leveled at them.

A grin crossed the sheriff's face. "Looks like you won't be alone on the gallows tomorrow, Mr. Roche."

Behind her, Aggie felt her father's fingers in her belt.

"Three," he whispered.

"What was that?" the sheriff called, as Aggie counted three and dove to the side.

The sheriff froze, struck by indecision. That was all the time Roche needed to aim and fire Aggie's derringer.

A hole appeared in the sheriff's shoulder, and he instinctively reached for it. Aggie pulled her revolver and fired three quick rounds. The first went high, piercing the lawman's ear. Settling down, the second hit him in the neck, sending blood flowing down the front of his shirt. By then, his fight or flight instinct had kicked in, and he was trying to bring his gun into play.

Aggie's last shot drilled him through the left eye, sending a splatter of blood and brain matter onto the wall behind him.

His gun clattered to the floor as he stood there for a moment, frozen in shock, before collapsing to the floor himself. Roche pushed the cell door open, derringer still raised.

Stepping to the desk, Roche checked the drawers until he found his gun belt. Strapping it on, he handed the derringer back to Aggie, who was reloading her pistol.

"Nice shooting," she said, tucking it back into the holster at the small of her back.

"Damned lucky to hit him at all with that peashooter," he growled.

As Roche took his carbine from the rack, Aggie went to the door and peeked outside. No one was running toward the sheriff's office, alarmed at the shooting. She guessed the thick walls had muffled the sound of the gunshots.

"You ready?" Roche asked.

Slipping around the building, she led him to where the horses were tied.

Behind her, Roche laughed.

"Only you would tie the damn horses to the gallows."

Aggie shrugged. "I gave the gallows a coal oil bath. Figured a fuego might be useful."

Untying the horses, they swung into the saddle. Roche lit a match and tossed it onto the wood, igniting the accelerant before they rode out of town.

Chapter 12

ROCHE

Three miles out of town, the road cut into a canyon. Roche rode through it lost in thought, deciding his next move now that he'd escaped the gallows.

Aggie had done well. She had a good head on her shoulders, no doubt from her mother, and she absorbed everything he'd taught her.

Sometimes it felt like he was just in her way.

He looked over his shoulder, and realized she wasn't behind him anymore.

Ahead of him, a match flashed, and a lantern appeared.

Roche reined in his horse, looking into the darkness and realizing he was surrounded.

"Well, well," Ray Spencer said, an evil grin crossing his face. "Look who came out to play."

Hooves sounded behind Roche, but he kept his eyes on Spencer.

"Where's your partner?" Spencer asked.

"What do you mean?"

Spencer shook his head. "I ain't stupid."

"Never said you were," Roche replied, looking around the circle for an opening.

"Talked to a couple fellows who were in the saloon. They said James had you dead to rights when you had your gun on Earl, then his head got plowed. So I checked your guns before you woke up yesterday. You didn't kill three men by firing two bullets."

Roche shrugged. "Funny things happen in places like this, you know?"

Spencer glared, and for a moment, Roche thought he might kill him then and there.

"Get off the horse," he finally ordered. "Landry, Curtis, take his guns and put him in the wagon."

"What about his partner?" one of the men asked.

Spencer shook his head. "I don't give a damn about the partner. This asshole is the one I want."

CHAPTER 13

AGGIE

A hundred yards away, Aggie peeked over the top of a boulder.

It was too far to try anything. In the dark, she was as likely to hit Roche as to take down one of Spencer's goons.

She knew it was Spencer. It had to be. Who else would be waiting for them in the dark?

As she watched, two of the goons finished searching Roche, then they tied him up and lifted him into the wagon.

Maybe she could get them in a rush, ride in with guns blazing and grab Roche before they knew what hit them.

No, that was suicide. There were too many of them, and in the darkness, the one she didn't see would be her undoing.

Aggie knew where they'd take Roche. She'd head there and wait.

Spencer barked an order, and the group moved farther into the canyon, the lantern fading in the distance.

"Well, hello."

Aggie turned to find a man standing over her.

"Spencer done said that asshole had a partner. Looks like he was right."

The man's gun was still in his holster.

Fool.

The knife was in her hand a moment later, and she lunged for his throat. He tried to step back, but tripped over his feet and she was on him. Slicing through muscle and tissue, blood spurted from his neck as the man's heart tried to get blood to his brain.

Within seconds, he was dead.

Wiping the knife on his pants, Aggie returned it to the sheath. Looking around to make sure he'd been the only straggler, she made her way back to where she'd hidden her horse.

Riding out of the canyon, she saw the flames from the gallows in the distance. The fire had spread to the jail, and she could hear the shouts of the men working to extinguish it.

That'd keep them busy.

Spurring her horse, she rode away from the canyon mouth, toward the trail that would save her a day's ride.

CHAPTER 14
TIDWELL

T idwell opened his eyes to the sound of hoofbeats. The screaming house was so isolated, anyone coming or going meant news. Most days, it was just him and the Doctor here, now that Spencer had run out of things to do to him.

The Doctor got to his feet and went outside. Tidwell heard him speaking to the new arrival, then the door opened as the Doctor returned.

"Looks like we'll be having a new guest soon," the Doctor said.

"What do you mean?"

The Doctor shook his head. "A sad thing. Ray's brothers were killed in town a couple days ago. Last night, the killer made a break for it. If Ray can get his hands on the bastard who did it, their screams will echo here for eternity."

"I hope I can meet him," Tidwell said. "I'd like to shake the man's hand."

The Doctor glared into the cell, and Tidwell wondered if there was a hell they hadn't put him through yet. Finally, the Doctor shook his head. "If you think what we did to you was awful, you can't imagine what we're going to do to him."

Tidwell wanted to laugh. There was nothing worse than what Spencer and the Doctor had done to him. Day after day, they'd pushed him to the limits of pain and endurance. Multiple times, he'd thought one more blow, one more ache, would send him over the edge into the depths of insanity, but they always managed to stop in time.

They knew a man's limits.

Tidwell didn't want to think about how they'd learned.

CHAPTER 15

AGGIE

The sheriff had been in Aggie's bed hours before she killed him.

"Hot damn," he'd said, collapsing to the sheets. "You know how to treat a man."

Aggie smiled, running a finger down his broad chest. "Someone's gotta take care of the law. Especially with you hanging that dangerous criminal tomorrow."

He laughed. "That boy won't be no trouble. Just a hired gun, thinks he's hot shit. He'll go out kickin' just like the rest of 'em."

"Still." She rubbed her breasts against him. "I like seeing justice done. It makes me all hot and bothered."

The sheriff grinned. "Maybe I'll come see you again tomorrow."

"I'd like that." Aggie twirled her hair around a finger. "It was so scary, watching what happened last night. I thought he was going to go crazy."

A shake of the head. "Nah. Perkins took care of him. He should have known better than to kill them boys. I run a tight ship around here, with no room for vigilante bounty hunters and their bullshit."

"Too bad for him."

"Yeah. He's gettin' off easy though. If Ray Spencer'd got hold of him, he'd have gone out to the Screaming House."

Aggie traced a finger around his cock, earning a shiver of pleasure. "What's the Screaming House?"

"That'd be Ray Spencer's personal torture chamber. Nothing you need to worry your pretty head about."

She smiled. "I heard Ray likes it rough."

A snort. "That's putting it mildly. He's a fucking pervert is what he is. Can't get off unless someone's screaming. If he didn't have the money he does, I'd have hung his ass long ago. But he behaves in town, and that's all I really care about. Truth is, I'm kinda glad that asshole killed his brothers. They were the troublemakers. With them gone, I ain't got a problem in the world."

"Except the Screaming House," Aggie reminded him.

The sheriff shook his head. "That ain't a problem. As long as I don't have to hear about it, I don't care what Ray does out on his ranch. Ain't like anyone misses them drifters and whores anyway."

Aggie pouted. "I hope you'd miss me."

He smiled. "You're too damn pretty for Ray to bother."

"Where is the Screaming House?" Aggie asked. "I don't want to run into it by accident."

The sheriff laughed. "Unless you end up out at the Spencer spread, you won't be anywhere near it. There's an old trail up past the canyon road we use sometimes when we need to get a message to Ray in a hurry, but you'd have to be real lost to end up at the Screaming House."

Aggie shivered. "I hate to think that hell is so close."

He'd reached for her breast, a smile crossing his face. "Luckily, heaven is closer."

Chapter 16
ROCHE

It was hotter than hell inside the wagon.

Roche lay on the hard wood, feeling the sun beat down on the cloth cover. His head still hurt from when Perkins had smashed his skull, and his throat was parched. There was no telling how long he'd been out there, or how much longer it would be before Spencer and his assholes woke up.

He tried to stretch out, but he was wedged among the rest of the wagon's cargo, and moving made his joints scream in pain.

There was no one around. They'd all scattered when they arrived at the Spencer spread, not even bothering to post a guard to make sure he stayed put.

Finally, he heard movement outside the wagon, the grumbles and curses of recently awoken men.

"Where the fuck is Vince?" he heard Spencer ask.

Silence.

"Where the fuck is Vince?"

"Hell, I swore he was here last night," another voice said.

"It was dark, must have seen someone else," someone added.

"Probably rode on to town," someone joked.

"Fucking hell," Spencer said. "Vince knows better than to ride off without a reason. If he ain't here, he's dead."

"What?" The wagon cover was thrown back, and strong hands yanked Roche into a sitting position.

"Where's your fucking partner?" one of Spencer's men demanded.

Roche tried to shrug. "No idea."

"He killed my brother!"

A fist slammed into Roche's head, and he felt blood flowing from a cut over his eye. Someone was pulling on his shirt, and Roche realized the other cowhands were trying to pull his assailant away.

Spencer grabbed the front of the assailant's shirt and yanked him away from the wagon. "Calm down, Rich."

"That's my brother you're saying is dead! I'm gonna kill this asshole, then I'm going to find his partner and kill him too!"

Ray had fire in his eyes. "Your fool brother went off alone in the dark, knowing there was another man out there. If he got himself killed, that's his own damn fault." He took a deep breath. "Apparently, this bastard's partner is more dangerous than we thought. If he got Vince, he can get the rest of us.

Johnny, Carlo, Sandoval, you three ride back toward town. See if you can pick up the sidewinder's trail and run him down."

"What do we do if we find 'um?"

"Bring him to the Screaming House."

Roche watched as the men headed for the corral. They were big men, brutes, but from the looks of them, he knew Aggie could outsmart the three of them put together.

But where the hell was she?

He remembered her next to him as they rode into the canyon. Somewhere between the entrance and the ambush, she'd managed to slip into a hiding spot.

That didn't surprise him. She was observant as hell, especially in the dark. He figured she'd expected trouble, and noticed something that gave her pause. The best chance for both of them was with her free.

It didn't mean he was happy in the nest of vipers, but he liked his odds better since she wasn't there with him.

Ray took out a canteen and held it out to him.

"Drink."

Taking it in his bound hands, Roche thought about hurling it at one of them, but instead lifted it to his lips. The water was brown and silty, but also the sweetest thing he'd ever tasted.

As he drank, he looked around. Spencer had four men left, now that the search party had ridden out. Vince's brother was glaring at him, and Roche had a feeling if the man got a chance, he'd take his grief out on him.

Spencer snatched the canteen from his hands, spilling water down the front of Roche's clothes. "That's enough." He looked around. "You boys keep a close eye on him now. He's dangerous."

"Hell," one of the men, a lanky man missing an ear, spoke up. "He's trussed up so good, I don't think he's going nowhere."

Spencer glared at the man. "He's smarter than you idiots put together. Watch his eyes, damn it. He's always looking for an opportunity, and if you give him one, you'll be joining Vince in the graveyard."

"It won't help him at the Screaming House," one of the others said, drawing laughter.

For a moment, Spencer glared at them, then allowed a grin. "Nope. It won't help him a bit."

CHAPTER 17

AGGIE

Aggie crouched on the ridgeline, looking down into the box canyon.

Raising her field glasses, she studied the building in the distance. The sawmill was all that was left of the old lumber camp, at the edge of a small clearing. Abandoned logs were scattered around the edge. In the center, a t-shaped structure stood, like a clothesline post without anything tied to it. Dark stains stood out against the sun-bleached wood, making her wonder what the thing was used for.

She was hidden across the canyon from where she'd left her horse. It was hobbled in a grove of trees, with a patch of grass and a small stream. If anyone came looking for her, they'd look there.

Not here, a quarter-mile across the canyon.

Using the field glasses, Aggie followed the road away from the mill until it disappeared in the distance. She'd see them coming from a long way off.

If she had a rifle, she could pick them off as they approached, bouncing from hiding place to hiding place, slowly improving the odds.

But if she did that, they might just shoot Roche and ride away.

That was the last thing she wanted.

So she'd have to be patient.

Crouching, she moved farther along the ridge.

A rattle sounded at her feet. Less than a second later, her knife pierced the snake's head, killing it instantly.

Damn snakes.

Finding a small overhang to protect her from the sun, she checked for snakes before taking a seat, pulling her canteen out for a drink.

The last snake had startled her.

But Aggie had always had the gift of stillness. Roche said she was better than the Indian scouts he'd ridden with in the cavalry, high praise from him.

The snake probably hadn't realized she was there until it was too late.

With luck, the snakes in the canyon would have the same experience.

CHAPTER 18

TIDWELL

H e missed Millie.

Maybe he'd join her in death, if there was a heaven like the preacher said.

Or, the way they'd lived, maybe they'd end up in hellfire together.

Tidwell remembered the first time he'd seen her, brown curls dancing down onto her plump curves, red lips open in a hearty laugh. She'd been on the balcony of Delilah's saloon, talking to another girl.

He'd walked up to her, wallet open, and told her he had to have her, right then, and she could name her price.

The next month had been expensive, but worth it. Millie had broadened his sexual horizons in ways Tidwell hadn't thought possible, but he'd come to value even more the post-coital glow, lying in her narrow bed together just talking and laughing before falling asleep next to each other.

Being with her was worth paying for the full night.

Finally, as he reached for his wallet one morning, she put her hand on his.

"No charge."

"What?"

Millie smiled. "I want to fuck you as much as you want to fuck me. Doesn't seem fair to charge you anymore."

That day, he'd helped her move from the saloon to his house.

"Dusty," she said, looking around the living room.

"I haven't spent much time here lately," he said.

Millie laughed. "Gee, I wonder why."

Two days later, he found out about the Screaming House.

He'd watched as two of Spencer's cowhands dragged a drunk from the alley next to Delilah's, throwing him into the back of a wagon.

One of the cowhands saw him and laughed. "Don't worry about it, Banker. He's got a special job to do for Ray!"

A deputy, watching from the hotel steps, looked away, and Tidwell caught him as the wagon bounced toward the ranch.

The deputy told him everything.

It took four months to siphon enough of Ray's money to leave. Tidwell did it carefully, small amounts of cash no one would miss hidden under a floorboard in his office.

If one of the tellers hadn't had aspirations for Tidwell's job, he'd have made his escape with Millie.

Instead, Ray's cowboys came bursting into their home the night before they planned to leave. Tidwell tried to fight, but when they put a gun to Millie's head, he surrendered.

The next thing he knew, he was in the back of a wagon, bouncing across the prairie to the Screaming House.

Now, he was about to die.

He wished Millie was here.

He wanted to hold her.

When she was in his arms, everything was okay.

CHAPTER 19

ROCHE

The road to the Screaming House was rough.

Every bounce, every pothole, sent Roche airborne in the back of the wagon. The cargo moved with him, sometimes slamming into his body, sometimes sliding beneath it to give him a painful landing.

At least nothing hit the same spot every time. His bruises were well distributed.

There was still no sign of Aggie. He figured she was somewhere nearby, watching and waiting for an opportunity to strike. She had good instincts, almost as good as his own, and though she lacked the benefit of twenty years in the Cavalry to hone them, she made up for it with boldness.

She made for a hell of an ace in the hole.

Another bump sent him airborne, and he landed hard on his shoulder, making him cry out in pain.

"Comfortable?" Spencer called from his horse.

They'd left the cover off the wagon, the sun beating down on him to make a hard journey even worse.

"This is like riding in a fucking Pullman!" Roche shot back. "When's the meal service?"

Spencer laughed. "We got a few hours yet before we reach our destination."

"And what happens there?"

The asshole grinned. "I'd hate to spoil the surprise."

Another bump. A crate slammed into Roche's head, and he fell unconscious.

CHAPTER 20

AGGIE

Aggie saw them coming from her hole on the canyon rim.

Six men. Add that to the two she'd seen down at the Screaming House, and it made eight.

Not great odds. But she'd seen worse. The trick was to avoid fighting them as a group, to pick them off one or two at a time until the odds were manageable.

Then you ruined their whole day.

She'd let them get to the Screaming House and get comfortable while she worked on her plan to draw them out.

CHAPTER 21
ROCHE

R oche woke as the wagon jerked to a stop.

"Get him out," he heard Spencer order.

Rough hands grabbed him and lifted him out of the wagon.

The first thing he saw was the post in the center of the clearing. The dark stains stood out even more close up, and the human bones scattered among the sawdust at the base turned his stomach.

"You like it?"

Roche spit at the base of the post. "I think it's fucking sick."

The men laughed.

"Don't worry," Spencer said, grinning. "You've got a long time before you end up here."

A man appeared at the door of the mill. He wore a leather apron, and the sleeves of his shirt showed faded bloodstains.

"Mr. Spencer," he nodded, before turning his eyes to Roche. "A new arrival?"

"Dr. Chapman, meet Mr. Roche, our newest guest." Spencer sounded like they were friends gathering at a hunting camp, not an isolated torture house. "Is Mr. Tidwell feeling better?"

"Almost perfect." The Doctor pulled out a pipe. Striking a match on his thumbnail, he lit the tobacco, making sure the match was extinguished before tossing it to the ground. "Certainly ready for anything you have in mind."

Spencer looked to the others. "Bring him out."

Three of them disappeared inside. They returned, two of them leading another man while the third carried a coil of rope and a small bag.

Tidwell looked at Roche, his eyes begging for help. He was at least forty, the sun reflecting off his bald head. His chest and back were covered in scars, each standing out against his pale skin.

"Back up the wagon," Spencer ordered.

Tidwell was lifted onto the tailgate, the rope passed under his arms and the ends thrown over the crossbeams.

Two of the henchmen used the rope to hoist Tidwell out of the wagon.

"He'd say something, but I cut out his tongue," Spencer explained, climbing into the wagon and opening the bag. Reaching in, he pulled out a hammer and a railroad spike, causing Roche to shudder.

"No taste for blood, Roche?" Spencer asked. "It didn't seem to bother you when you killed my brothers."

"That was justice. This is madness."

Spencer grinned. "This is justice, justice for those who understand civilization is its own form of insanity. Tidwell was my banker, until I noticed my accounts didn't add up, and had an audit performed. His mistake was incalculable, but will soon be rectified."

"By killing him."

Spencer nodded. "Of course. If I didn't, he might do it again."

The henchmen pulled Tidwell into place on the cross as Spencer took the man's arm. Raising the hammer, he drove a spike into the man's wrist.

Tidwell screamed.

When he finished the other arm, Spencer hopped off the wagon as the rope was pulled away, leaving Tidwell suspended. His feet balanced on a thin piece of wood nailed to the post, holding his body up as best they could.

"Crucifixion," Spencer said, approaching Roche. "It's where we get the word 'excruciating.' And that's what it is: hours exposed to the elements, trying to keep your feet balanced on that piece of wood, knowing when you slip off it, the pain will increase, and death will soon follow. And you're conscious the whole time, thinking about it, knowing what's coming. But no matter how strong you are, eventually, you'll fall."

Roche looked up at Tidwell, the pain and desperation on the man's face apparent. "Seems barbaric."

"Perhaps," Spencer said, nodding agreement. "But effective, nonetheless." He gestured to the cross. "Now you've seen your destination. But there is a long road for you before the cross."

CHAPTER 22

AGGIE

In her hiding spot, Aggie lowered her field glasses. Jesus Christ! A cross?

Fuck them all!

A flash of movement caught her eye, and she gazed across the canyon. Three riders had appeared on the trail that had brought her there. She watched as they reached the edge, stopping to look around. One barked orders, then continued down the trail, riding toward the Screaming House as the other two dismounted. Spreading out, they began to look around.

Looking in the wrong place, pendejos, Aggie thought as she slid farther under the overhang.

CHAPTER 23

TIDWELL

When they brought Tidwell to the Screaming House, they'd blindfolded him when they got close, taking great pains to only let him see the inside.

When Spencer's cowboys dragged him outside, he'd realized they weren't extending the new man the same courtesy.

They'd made him watch as Spencer drove railroad spikes through Tidwell's wrists and left him hanging on the cross.

Spencer was a fucking bastard.

They were all fucking bastards.

And he'd kill them yet, Spencer, the Doctor, and anyone else he could get his hands on.

Crucifixion. Only Spencer would think to bring this ancient method into the modern world.

Christ, his wrists hurt.

Someone had nailed a board to the cross at Tidwell's feet, and as long as he could balance on it, he could breathe.

He hoped he wouldn't fall off.

It would hurt like hell to climb back on, with only his wrists to support his weight.

If he could climb back on, that is.

CHAPTER 24

ROCHE

Roche was placed in a cell in the corner of what looked like an office. Across the room, a desk and chair sat in the corner, and a bed was on the far wall. Between the bed and desk were a pair of wooden cabinets.

The door opened, and Dr. Chapman stepped in.

Up close, a jagged scar running from his eyebrow to his chin was apparent. Part of his ear was missing, and at his hairline, Roche could see another scar. His nose had been broken, probably more than once.

He didn't look like a doctor as much as a prizefighter.

Chapman stood in front of the cell, far enough away that Roche couldn't grab him, but close enough to study him.

"Have you figured out your fate?"

Roche nodded. "They tear me apart, you patch me up. When they're done, I go out to the cross."

"Exactly!" Chapman clapped his hands together. "My job is to let them take you to the brink of death, but not so far I can't piece you back together."

Roche spit onto the floor in front of the Doctor. "And you call yourself a medical professional?"

Chapman chuckled. "I'm no ordinary medical professional. My work here has elevated medicine in ways most doctors will never understand. Experimental medicine at its finest."

"With Spencer's victims as your lab rats?" Roche sat on the bed. Even with the time he'd spent unconscious, the trip had been tiring.

"They don't mind. Some of them are even grateful, believe it or not. After the pain Ray doles out, my work can bring a measure of relief."

Roche shook his head. "Where the fuck did Spencer find you?"

"Ogden," the Doctor replied simply. "My career started in St. Louis, but a jealous husband led to my sudden departure. Fortunately, the war was starting, and I disappeared into the Confederate service. I mostly served in the west. After Atlanta, I slipped away, not wanting to be chased across Georgia by that bastard Sherman. I wound up at a place called Andersonville."

Roche's eyes narrowed. "I've heard of Andersonville. They said it was hell."

A grin crept across Chapman's face. "Not quite, though I did my best. By then, the guards knew the war was lost, and wanted a measure of revenge. I provided it, and managed to slip away a week before the Yankees liberated it."

"You rat bastard," Roche growled. "You sadistic piece of shit!"

Chapman laughed. "That's a wonderful compliment! From Andersonville, I made my way across the south, hiding in the scars of the reconstruction, passing on as the situation became untenable. I was known as a man who would do anything, for the right price. Castrations, abortions, even torture. My services were always in demand."

"So how'd you end up here?" Roche asked. "Finally run out of places to hide?"

He nodded. "Pretty damn close. I got chased out of the Indian Territory, and decided to try my luck out west. I woke up in an Ogden hotel room to find Ray Spencer sitting next to my bed. He asked if the rumors he'd heard were true."

"You should have told him to go fuck himself."

More laughter. "How do you think Ray Spencer would have taken that? I told him it was true, and he offered me a job. That was eight years ago. Been here ever since."

Roche shook his head. "You're as insane as he is."

Chapman sighed. "Tell me, if you woke up tomorrow unable to perform, would you try anything to be able to fuck again?"

Roche raised an eyebrow. "What the fuck does that have to do with anything?"

"Just answer the question."

Roche shook his head. "There's a lot of anything I couldn't do. Fucking isn't worth some things."

An eyebrow raised. "You're lying to yourself."

"No."

He shrugged. "No matter. Ray Spencer is sick. He knows he's sick. Poor bastard needs extreme stimuli to get it up."

"Torture," Roche said.

"Exactly. At first it was mild, but as time has passed, he's needed more drastic measures to be satisfied."

"You say that like it's a medical condition," Roche challenged. "It's fucking sick."

"But you know any normal man would do anything he could for sexual release. Spencer just happens to have the money, space, and influence to pull it off."

Roche hated himself for thinking this cretin might have a point. He'd never admit it to this piece of shit, but over the years, he'd drifted into a whorehouse from time to time, needing the release that only physical intimacy could provide. Though he told himself it didn't mean anything, it was a need, and a need he couldn't meet on his own.

If he couldn't experience it anymore, he'd probably consider doing exactly what Spencer was doing. Then he'd blow his brains out for being willing to do that to another person.

He realized Chapman was studying him through the bars.

"Deny it all you want," the Doctor said. "If you were in his shoes, you'd do what he's doing, and you know it."

As Chapman left the room, Roche couldn't shake the thought that even as tired as he was, it would be hard to sleep that night.

The nightmares would keep him up.

CHAPTER 25

AGGIE

As the sun set, Aggie slipped along the canyon rim, staying in the shadows as much as she could. There was no way anyone could see her from the canyon floor, but she wasn't taking any chances.

At the Screaming House, one man was outside. She could see the glow of his cigarette as he sat on the building's porch.

The two men who'd been searching for her had gone down to the Screaming House just before she set out, leading her horse.

Good. They'd take care of it until she was ready to retrieve it.

Aggie hadn't heard any screaming from inside the building. She hadn't even heard anything from the man on the cross, who had to be in the worst pain of his life.

She remembered a sermon from the priest back in Ojinaga, years and miles in her past.

"We cannot imagine the pain our Lord endured on the cross, trying to breathe as the nails dug into his wrists and ankles. He did this for us, for our salvation..."

The memory was worth a chuckle. Aggie had made her own salvation, far from the priest and his adobe church.

For a moment, she considered slipping down the trail to the sawmill. She'd kill the sentry and be away before they knew what hit them.

But she knew that was folly. They were still looking for her, and they would be back up here tomorrow to keep searching. If she slipped into their camp, it would put them on the defensive, and she needed to increase her odds before she could take the fight to them.

So she'd spend the night preparing, and come morning, she'd pick them off one by one.

The only downside was while she was hunting, Roche would be hurting.

CHAPTER 26
TIDWELL

The assholes were looking for someone.

A group of riders arrived at sundown, picking their way down a trail in the canyon wall, leading an extra horse. He heard them talking to Ray on the porch, telling the asshole they'd tracked a rider from near town to the edge of the cliffs, where they'd lost them.

Someone else was out there.

The pain was mostly gone now, the sharp pangs having settled to dull aches.

Unless he moved his arms. Then lightning shot from his wrists to his core, and he had to fight the urge to pull his arms in.

Tidwell wished he could put the Doctor here in his place, kick back on the porch, and drink something cold as he watched the Doctor struggle.

The Doctor wouldn't last long. Maybe an afternoon. He was good at inflicting pain, but couldn't handle it himself.

Not like Spencer. Spencer would last a week out of spite, then another because he was a pure bastard. When Spencer told the new arrival about the record, he'd almost sounded disappointed.

Six days.

Tidwell intended to give the record a hell of a challenge, in hopes Spencer would beat him to the gates of hell.

CHAPTER 27

AGGIE

ggie woke as the sun rose over the mountains behind her. From her new hiding place, a nest of fallen branches at the edge of the canyon, she could see the man on the cross was still moving.

She wondered how long it would take him to die.

She wondered how he found the will to stay alive.

If it was her on the cross, she'd be doing anything she could to hasten her death. But the man nailed to it seemed determined to fight, as if he knew there was someone out there coming to save him.

Hope. The last refuge of the damned.

Smoke rose from the chimney, and Aggie figured they were making breakfast. Soon, they'd be coming after her.

Two men had been at the Screaming House.

Six had arrived with Roche.

Three had followed her through the mountains.

That made the current odds eleven to one.

She wondered how much she could even them before sundown.

CHAPTER 28

ROCHE

"Good morning."

Dr. Chapman led the small procession into the torture room. Behind him, a pair of guards forced Roche inside. Bringing up the rear, another outlaw carried a shotgun in case Roche somehow got loose.

The room they entered was the same size as the one with Roche's cell. He wondered where all the sawmill equipment had gone, but realized its absence may have been a good thing. Fewer toys for Spencer to use.

In the center of the room, a horizontal cross was waiting. After Roche removed his clothes, his escorts helped him onto it, using leather straps to secure his arms and legs.

He supposed he could have resisted, but at this point, all that would have done was waste energy. Roche wasn't sure how many men Spencer had here, but the three he saw, ugly bruisers picked for brawn more than brains, looked like enough to handle him.

Besides, his head still hurt.

Roche turned his head to see Spencer standing next to a cloth-covered table. He figured Spencer would whip away the cloth with a flourish, revealing a variety of nasty surprises.

Spencer himself was dressed as the Doctor had been yesterday, a leather apron covering his clothes. Stepping forward, he looked down, studying his canvas.

"This room is strange, Roche," he finally said. "The folks I expect to last tend to break the quickest. At the same time, the ones that seem weak often last longer than I think even I could endure. Take Mr. Tidwell, for instance. He survived seventeen days in the Screaming House, four short of the record. I'm interested to see how long he lasts on the cross."

"What's the record for that?" Chapman asked, returning to the table in his own apron.

"Six days, that preacher's wife. She called down every kind of damnation and hellfire she could think of before she finally died."

Roche laughed. "Get ready for a new record, if you live long enough."

Now Spencer smiled. "Ah, yes, your vanishing partner. They trailed him to the canyon rim above us. I've sent out some men

Bits of bone stuck out of the ripped skin as blood flowed from every orifice. The worst part was their heads, smashed beyond recognition, gray brains surrounding them like halos.

A gunshot rang out, chipping the rock next to her as she ducked back.

They'd seen her.

So some had survived.

Drawing her gun, she ran toward the woods. She wasn't sure how many had been killed, but she knew her odds were improving.

CHAPTER 30

ROCHE

S pencer took a branding iron from the fire and held it over Roche.

"This is going to hurt," he said with a smile.

"Try turning me loose before you do that," Roche shot back.

Spencer and Chapman looked at each other, then laughed. "I think I'll pass." Raising the iron, Spencer rammed it into Roche's thigh.

Roche tried not to scream, tried not to give them the satisfaction, but the burning pain was too much. He lost track of time, closing his eyes and tensing his body in the hope the pain would go away.

Finally, he opened his eyes to see Spencer and Chapman looking down at him.

Both men were grinning.

"Maybe you won't break the record after all," Spencer said.

CHAPTER 31

AGGIE

The sound of the scream distracted Aggie for a moment, but then she got her head together. They may be hurting Roche, but she couldn't help him until she evened the odds a little more.

Three men climbed out of the canyon, guns drawn. One of them was limping, using his rifle as a cane.

"I want the son-of-a-bitch," he growled, looking around as they spread out, making it impossible for her to get them all in one burst.

They were exposed, in the open, wanting her to fire so they could pinpoint her location.

She wasn't going to give them the satisfaction.

"Spread out," the limper ordered. "Don't forget, Spencer wants him alive."

Aggie grinned. Too bad for them she didn't want the same.

Chapter 32

TIDWELL

G unshots on the ridge.

Screams from inside.

Tidwell wanted to believe help was still coming. But it was hard, harder with each passing moment.

Six men had left the screaming house shortly after dawn, climbing the trail leading to the top of the ridge.

Six against one.

As a money man, Tidwell didn't like those odds.

He hadn't slept a wink. Every time he started to drift off, his wrists rubbed against the spikes, sending bolts of pain through his arms.

Instead of sleeping, he'd spent the night reimagining what he'd do to the Doctor. As the darkness wore on, his ideas became more and more perverted and painful. He'd use one torture per day, until the Doctor finally cracked.

Just like Spencer and the Doctor had done to him.

Tidwell had no idea how long he'd been at the Screaming House. Between the time he'd spent unconscious and delirious with pain, an accurate count was impossible. But it felt like the tortures had lasted an eternity, leaving him a broken shell of a man. Nothing in his body worked right. Most of his bones had been broken, and the ones that hadn't still ached from the other tortures.

Then, as he was nursed back to health, the Doctor took every chance he could to remind him the worst was yet to come.

The Doctor was wrong.

This wasn't the worst.

And if the person on the ridge was still alive, he might survive this yet.

Chapter 33
ROCHE

Roche looked at his left hand, his pinky attached by nothing more than a sliver of skin.

He hadn't screamed this time, as Spencer pulled it back until the bone finally snapped, the sharp end piecing the skin, allowing it to tear as Spencer kept applying pressure.

Spencer stepped back, allowing Chapman to step in and staunch the bleeding.

No anesthesia. No ether. Roche would have to endure the pain of breaking and the pain of fixing.

Behind the Doctor, Spencer had his dick out and was stroking it, staring at the wound with a strange glimmer in his eyes.

"Is that all it takes to get you off?" Roche gasped as the Doctor applied a hot iron to cauterize the wound.

"It's the anticipation." Spencer moaned as his seed shot onto the wooden floor. "That was just a taste of what was coming."

Stepping to the table, he finally removed the sheet with a flourish, revealing metal implements of various shapes and sizes. From where he was lying, Spencer could see knives, saws, drills, and things he didn't recognize.

"A broken pinky is nothing compared to what I have planned," Spencer said, his eyes moving over the instruments.

Chapman stepped back. "The pinky is fixed."

Spencer turned, holding a pair of metal pliers. "Then we'll have to break something else."

CHAPTER 34

AGGIE

The limper was walking straight toward her, as the other two moved away along the canyon rim.

Slipping farther into the woods, Aggie crouched behind a tree. She heard a twig snap as he entered the woods.

He moved past the tree without seeing her, and she grabbed his rifle. Without it to support him, he tumbled to the ground, and she was on him before he could make a sound.

Holding a hand over his mouth, she pulled her knife with the other and slashed it across his neck.

Blood spurted out, a spray hitting Aggie in the face. Resisting the urge to wipe it away, she kept her hand over his mouth as his body bucked, trying to throw her off so he could try to save himself.

Finally, he went still, the dark wound no longer pouring out blood.

Aggie turned to look at the rifle, and saw a shadow.

Fuck.

One of the others had slipped up behind her while she was dealing with the limper.

His hand was already going for his gun as Aggie reached for hers. He fired as she brought her gun up, the bullet slamming into her arm. Steadying her hand, she fought the pain to aim and pull the trigger.

Her aim was true, the bullet hitting his right eye and exploding out the back of his skull, ripping a path through his brain that caused him to collapse to the ground.

Fuck, her arm hurt.

But there was still another one out there, and he'd be looking for her, drawn by the sound of the gunfire.

She crept to the edge of the woods and looked out.

There he was, running toward her. His gun was out, but he hadn't seen her yet. With her injured arm, she'd have to wait until there was no way to miss.

Thank God it wasn't her gun hand.

He slowed to a walk, approaching carefully.

Fifty yards.

Thirty.

Twenty.

Ten.

As he finally saw her, she fired. The first round hit his shoulder, turning him away from her. She fired again, the bullet ripping through his arm and into his torso.

He tried to bring his gun up, but his hand refused to respond. The man turned toward her, and she could see the fear in his eyes.

She didn't care.

Taking careful aim, Aggie sent a bullet through his heart.

CHAPTER 35

ROCHE

Spencer looked up at the sound of gunfire.

"What the hell was that?" he asked.

"Sounded like shooting," Chapman replied, staring at the hand-powered drill in Spencer's hand. Spencer was guiding it into Roche's kneecap, having torn the nails off his toes.

"Carlo!" Spencer yelled.

A few moments later, one of the henchmen appeared in the doorway. "Yes, Boss?"

"Go watch the trail. If anyone but our boys come down, shoot 'em."

Carlo paused. "You think they're dead, sir?"

Spencer glared at him. "I don't know what the fuck I think, but I don't want any surprises."

Roche smiled in spite of his pain. Aggie was evening the odds.

Spencer looked down and saw the grin. Shaking his head, he turned the handle, and the drill cut into Roche's kneecap, erasing the smile and drawing a scream.

CHAPTER 36

AGGIE

Atop the ridge, Aggie was cutting off a piece of the dead man's shirt. It was tough, working with one hand, but she finally managed it.

Her own shirt lay on the ground nearby, the wound washed with water from her canteen. The bullet had passed through the flesh of her arm, not striking bone or blood vessel. It'd heal on its own, it'd just hurt for a while.

Wrapping the makeshift bandage around her arm, she winced as she pushed the cloth into the wound. Using her teeth and good arm, she managed to tie off the bandage to keep it in place.

Pulling on her own shirt, she struggled to button it with one hand, but finally succeeded.

Walking to her victims, she picked up the men's guns. Two carbines, a sawed-off shotgun, three pistols, and plenty of rounds.

She had herself an armory.

Walking to the edge of the canyon, she peeked over it.

A man was leaning against the corner of the Screaming House, watching the trail. He'd be waiting to find out what happened up here.

Death. Death had happened up here.

The last man was still alive under the second rock. Both his legs had been crushed, but his eyes were open as he glanced around.

Poor bastard. He'd be scared to death, hoping one of his friends would return to help him.

But they were all dead, and soon enough, he would be too.

Looking past the man at the corner, she saw the man on the cross was still alive. Surviving twenty-four hours was impressive as hell, she thought.

The Screaming House had five defenders left, and tonight, she'd go down to meet them.

CHAPTER 37

TIDWELL

It was silent on the ridge now.

There'd been a flurry of gunshots a few minutes ago. Six against one wasn't great odds, but whoever was up there was his only hope.

Tidwell would know soon. Either the men would return, or whoever was up there would continue their persecution of Spencer and his men.

The longer he hung here, the more he wanted to give up. He could feel insanity creeping at the edges of his mind, a desire to surrender to the heat and pain.

Looking down his arms, he could see the wounds around the spikes were red and inflamed. The pain was almost as bad as when they'd driven in the nails.

Infection.

The Doctor hated infection. In the Screaming House, he did everything he could to prevent it. He said infection killed more men than the actual injuries.

Tidwell had no idea if it was true. He just knew his wrists were infected now, and the Doctor was beyond caring.

God, he needed a drink, something to help fight off the heat.

The sun had started to descend in the sky. Tidwell hoped he could keep pushing the insanity away until it faded over the horizon and the cool night returned.

Another attack. His head clouded and the heat rolled through, trying to push his brain out of his skull.

He fought, thinking of the Doctor and Spencer. Tidwell wanted to watch them die, and that wouldn't happen if he went crazy.

His head cleared, but he felt weak.

Fighting the madness was costing him strength, as much or more than the infection.

"Hurry," he thought, wishing the fighter on the ridge would hear him.

CHAPTER 38

AGGIE

As the sun set over the far ridge, Aggie watched three men slip away from the Screaming House and into the woods around the cross.

An ambush.

If they'd waited for darkness, she wouldn't have seen them, and she wouldn't know what was coming.

Three in the woods, two in the Screaming House.

She peeked over the edge. The man under the boulder was dead, she could tell from here.

Vultures had started to arrive, congregating at the turn in the trail where the pancaked gunmen still lay. Two of them were picking at the one trapped under the boulder, their sharp beaks opening dark wounds in his flesh.

Behind Aggie, a pistol cocked.

"Hands up."

CHAPTER 39

ROCHE

Roche's knee was still throbbing in pain. He'd never walk without a limp, and that was if the damn leg didn't get infected and have to come off.

They probably wouldn't put him under for that either. The Doctor would get his saw and go to work.

He'd seen it before, during the war, doctors working as fast as they could to save what they could. The men screamed, but some of them survived the shock and horror of the amputation.

Roche remembered the piles of limbs outside the hospital, the stink of rotting flesh, and promising himself he'd blow his brains out before he let them take one of his limbs.

Now he might not have a choice.

Chapman and Spencer returned from their supper, and Chapman pulled the dressing off Roche's knee. Shaking his head, he went to a table in the corner and began assembling a poultice.

"Dr. Chapman is unconventional," Spencer said, standing at Roche's feet. "He doesn't just rely on modern medicine, he borrows from other sources. Native, Negro, anything he thinks might work, he tries it. More often than not, he succeeds. If he ever left here, he'd do things no one thought possible."

"If he left here, they'd hang his ass," Roche whispered.

In the corner, Chapman chuckled. "They've probably forgotten me."

"Not in Sunflower County, they haven't," Spencer replied with a grin.

"I didn't tell him that story yet," Chapman said.

"You should have," Spencer said. "Bunch of carpetbagging Yankees went down to reform Sunflower County. The local leaders didn't like that very much, and decided to teach them a lesson. You ever hear of a blood eagle?"

Roche shook his head.

"Supposedly the ancient Norse used it as a torture method. You break a man's ribs at the spine, then pull his lungs out to give the eagle its wings." Spencer grinned now, and reached for his cock. "I'd do it to you, but then I couldn't put you on the cross."

"The fat Yankee asshole I did it to, he screamed the whole time," Chapman said, carrying the completed poultice to Roche. "They paid me five thousand dollars to do it to him, then when I finished and they realized what I was capable of, they wanted me gone."

"Nailed him to the front door of the courthouse," Spencer grinned. "Best thing the Doctor could have done with a damn Yankee."

Chapman put the poultice on Roche's knee. At first, the weight made him gasp in pain, but as the cool fabric settled, it seemed to help.

"Thank you," he breathed, making Chapman smile.

"You may want to hold off on that," he said. "We've got one more item planned for tonight."

Roche's eyes narrowed.

"Don't worry, it's a relatively simple procedure," Spencer said, taking a knife from his belt. "Hope you don't mind singing soprano."

"Jesus! Fucking freak!" Roche twisted and turned, struggling against the leather straps.

Spencer reached for Roche's balls. "This is going to hurt."

CHAPTER 40

AGGIE

Aggie was trying to figure out who had gotten the drop on her. No one had come out of the canyon, but here she was, hands raised, with a gun on her. The voice sounded familiar too, but she couldn't place it.

"Put your hands behind your back, and if you even think about going for the gun on your hip, I'll blow your ass across the canyon."

Truthfully, she hadn't been thinking about the gun on her hip.

She'd been thinking about the derringer behind her belt.

Aggie heard the clink of metal, and knew he'd holstered his gun to handcuff her. A lawman? Out here? She wanted to laugh. Both the sheriff and his deputy were dead.

This was some wannabe.

What if there were two of them? She still might end up dead.

That was a risk she had to take.

As soon as she felt his hand touch hers, she pulled the derringer and fired blindly behind her.

Aggie heard a grunt, and turned, dropping the derringer and pulling her revolver. Pointing it at the center of the man, she fired twice.

He staggered, then fell to the ground, the last ray of sunlight glistening off the star on his chest.

She recognized him from town, a blowhard who'd talked big about his history as a marshal down in Texas. Apparently, they'd turned to him to replace the sheriff.

Poor choice.

She knelt next to him, and he looked up. "I know you," he gasped.

"You should." He'd paid for her two or three times.

"What are you doing out here?"

"I should ask you the same question." She looked over his wounds. The derringer had hit him in the gut, but her next two shots had hit him in the right lung. He was dying, but it would be slow.

"Need to find Ray Spencer," he gasped. "The Federal Marshal is coming for him. Told me to arrest him. He needs to get out of here." He coughed, blood pooling in his mouth. Trying to inhale, he choked on the blood. There wasn't anything Aggie could do but try to make him comfortable. A minute later, he was dead.

Looking down at his corpse, Aggie shook her head. "The only place Ray Spencer's going is hell."

CHAPTER 41

TIDWELL

As the sun began to set, Tidwell heard more gunshots from the ridge.

They helped push back the weight driving his sanity away, at least for a moment.

Spencer seemed to know the men he'd sent up the ridge hadn't survived. Three more men had emerged from the Screaming House, taking up positions in the woods around him.

If there was a crossfire, he'd be trapped in the middle.

No.

Whoever was on the ridge was too smart for that. They'd have been watching, seen the men take their hiding places, and planned their assault accordingly.

He missed Millie. He'd give anything to hold her again, to smell her hair, to kiss her soft lips before the last bit of sanity abandoned his mind.

Tidwell might even let Spencer and the Doctor live.

No, he decided, he wouldn't go that far.

He could only enjoy heaven with Millie knowing those two were in hell.

Heaven.

God, was that even possible after what he'd seen, what he'd failed to stop? He deserved to be in hell with Spencer and the Doctor.

At least he'd done what he could.

As the weight of insanity returned, he wondered if it would be enough.

Chapter 42

AGGIE

Aggie slipped down the path, maneuvering carefully past the boulder and the bodies.

The three men waiting for her were hoping to catch her as she went into the Screaming House, to cut her down in the open before she could do anything.

It wasn't a bad plan.

But Aggie knew where they were.

A dull throb came from her injured arm, and she was thankful again it wasn't her good arm.

She carried the sawed-off shotgun, a double-barrel model she'd taken off one of the fallen assholes. Since she expected a short-range fight, it was the best choice of the guns at her disposal.

Reaching the bottom of the cliff, she left the trail and slipped through the woods under the light of a half-moon. Treading lightly, she was almost noiseless, a shadow in the night.

Ahead of her, someone coughed.

Aggie peeked around a tree to see a man lying behind a log, rifle propped across it, aimed into the clearing.

Wrong way, cabrón.

Pulling her knife, she crept up behind him. This was the hard part. One wrong move, one noise to betray her, and she'd find herself under fire from three directions.

Putting her foot between the man's legs, she knelt on his back, grabbing his hair and yanking his head back with one hand as she slit his throat with the other.

He didn't have time to yell.

Blood poured onto the forest floor, reflecting the moonlight. Her victim squirmed, trying to break free, but she held him down until he went still.

One down, two to go.

CHAPTER 43

ROCHE

"Not a bad job, if I do say so," Chapman said, using a knife to cut the last bit of suture.

Roche looked at the pile of flesh on his chest, his balls and cock. The removal had hurt like hell, a hurt that went beyond physical pain and reached into the depths of his soul. Staring at the bloody appendage, he couldn't help but wonder if he was still a man.

Fuck, was he anything anymore?

This went beyond the pale. There were some things you just didn't do, even if you were going to kill someone.

Roche hoped before this was over, he'd get to return the favor for Spencer and Chapman.

"I've never figured out how they're supposed to piss," he heard Spencer say.

"Little bit of creative plumbing," Chapman replied. "Messy as hell, but they don't live long enough for it to matter."

Fuck. They'd done this before?

Of course they had. These assholes would do it to every man they got in this sick place.

Roche wondered what they did to women. Cut off their tits?

No. A woman wasn't as emotionally connected to her body the way a man was to his dick.

Fuck.

FUCK!

While he'd been lost in thought, Spencer had picked up a sledgehammer and slammed it into his uninjured knee.

He tried to reach for it, to curl his body into a fetal position to protect himself from more pain, but the straps held him in place.

"Just making sure you're awake," Spencer said with an evil grin.

"You ratshit motherfucker!" Roche gasped. "You're gonna get it just like your brothers."

Spencer laughed. "Maybe someday, but not today."

CHAPTER 44

AGGIE

Aggie found the second man standing behind a tree, peeking out at the clearing.

She crept up to him, carefully placing each footfall.

Behind her, an owl hooted.

Her target spun around, startled, and saw her.

Aggie's gun was in her hand a moment later, and she squeezed the trigger.

As the man fell, gunfire erupted from the trees across the clearing. Grabbing the dead man's rifle, she dove to the ground, her night vision destroyed by the muzzle flashes.

A shadow emerged from the tree line, running for the door of the Screaming House. Aggie waited, aiming for the steps.

As soon as she heard boots pounding on wood, she fired.

"Fuck!" came the yell.

Racking another round into the chamber, she fired again, then repeated the process a third time as the man fell to the ground.

"Ow! Jesus!" he yelled. "Doc! Get out here and help me, Goddamn you! I've been shot!"

Aggie watched the door, but no one appeared.

CHAPTER 45

ROCHE

"Sounds like someone's looking for you, Doc," Roche hissed. "Maybe you can cut his balls off too."

Spencer drove his fist into Roche's groin, and pain racked his body. Even without balls, getting hit there hurt. Picking up a shotgun, Spencer walked toward the door.

"Looks like I have to deal with this myself," he muttered as he went.

Chapman looked at Roche's groin, and shook his head.

"Gonna take some work to fix that."

"Maybe you can make it hurt a little more," Roche gasped.

"Like this?" Balling his hand into a fist, Chapman slammed it into Roche's drilled knee, drawing a scream.

"You sick bastard!" Roche hissed when the worst of the pain had passed.

Chapman laughed. "I am that, and more."

CHAPTER 46

TIDWELL

G unfire erupted from the woods around Tidwell.

He winced, knowing he was exposed, knowing one shot could finish him.

But it didn't come.

His arms and hands throbbed in pain as the infection moved out from his wrists.

The heat had boiled his brain, leaving him with a single thought: kill Spencer and the Doctor.

Behind him, footsteps.

Was it one of Spencer's men?

The fighter from the ridge?

At this point, he didn't care.

Tidwell just wanted to kill Spencer and the Doctor so he could die.

CHAPTER 47

AGGIE

Somehow, the man on the cross was still alive.

He was muttering something incoherent, his body refusing to give up as he stayed balanced on the block.

As she crept across the clearing, Aggie made a decision.

Climbing the support, she reached out, her fingers finding the rotting flesh where the spike had been driven through his wrist.

With a gentle push, the arm fell off the nail.

The next thing she knew, he was falling, landing in a heap at the foot of the cross.

Aggie dropped down, landing next to him and helping him to his feet. She let go of him, and he staggered, uncertain, but still alive enough.

"The stairs." She pointed.

He nodded, walking toward the Screaming House.

On the porch, a door swung open, the light from inside silhouetting a gunman.

Aggie raised the shotgun and fired.

The gunman disappeared.

She crept toward the porch, sure she'd hit him, but uncertain of the damage.

A figure reappeared, gun shouldered, aiming for her.

Something pushed her as the gunman fired. She fell to the ground, aiming the shotgun as she went. The second barrel boomed, and the gunman fell.

Drawing her pistol, Aggie put a round through the gunman's head before approaching the figure on the ground.

It was the crucified man, his chest shredded by the shotgun blast meant for her.

"Thanks," Aggie said. "I guess this is better than the cross."

Stepping over him, she climbed the steps and entered the Screaming House.

CHAPTER 48

TIDWELL

T idwell had taken the brunt of the shotgun blast, pushing his friend, his savior, to the ground.

It was the only choice. The few moments on his feet had shown him he was too weak to put up a fight, but they could still kill Spencer and the Doctor.

The wound didn't hurt. Nothing hurt.

Looking up, he saw the figure on the porch fall, and realized it was Spencer.

Only the Doctor was left.

As his friend stepped to the porch, he got a good look at them in the moonlight and gasped.

It was a woman, long hair flowing from under her hat, determination burning in her eyes.

Was she an angel?

As Tidwell closed his eyes for the last time, he hoped she was an angel of death.

Chapter 49

ROCHE

Roche looked up at the Doctor as the echo of the gunshots outside faded. "Looks like you're the only one left. Maybe you should go ahead and surrender."

The Doctor laughed. "You'd like that, wouldn't you?"

"Well," Roche said. "If you ain't gonna surrender, you might want to start getting right with the Lord, 'cuz you're fixing to meet him."

"Awfully confident for a man with no balls," the Doctor said, turning back to the table, looking over the tools.

Roche was silent. He'd almost forgotten what the Doctor had done, forgotten the dull pain from down there. Maybe he wanted to forget, to pretend it never happened. But part of him knew he never would.

He didn't want Aggie to find him like this, to see him like this. The father she'd never had, emasculated. But at the same time, he wanted to spend more time with his daughter, to talk about the moments he'd missed and enjoy life together.

But most of all, he wanted the Doctor, this sadistic fuck, dead. Dead so he couldn't hurt anyone else. The trail of pain and suffering ended here at the Screaming House.

He heard boots pounding in the hallway, and saw the Doctor take something from the table and hide it in his hand.

Chapter 50

AGGIE

Aggie found Roche strapped to a horizontal cross, the last defender of the Screaming House standing behind him.

"Hands up!" Aggie ordered, aiming her pistol at the man.

"No."

Roche turned his head and looked at Aggie. "Tell your mother I never stopped loving her."

"Tell her yourself," Aggie replied, staring down the Doctor. "I said hands up! I mean it! I'll shoot."

The Doctor laughed. "No, you won't."

Before she could do anything, his hand moved, and a thin red line appeared on Roche's neck. The flesh burst open, blood flowing down his skin and dripping onto the floor.

"I'm a doctor. I can save him," Chapman said, "but you have to put the gun down."

She glanced at Roche. God, she hadn't had enough time with him. He was looking at her now, sadness in his blue eyes, and his lips were moving.

"Kill him."

CHAPTER 51

ROCHE

Roche didn't even think about it.

The Doctor had to die, that he was sure of. If he somehow managed to escape, he'd haunt Roche for the rest of his life.

Or Roche would spend the rest of his life trying to track him down.

It wasn't what he wanted.

What he wanted was a life with Aggie, to go back to that village in Mexico and hold Ysidra again, to make up for the twenty years denied him by her father's lie.

But this man, this doctor, was worse than a killer. He tortured, he preyed on the weak, and he couldn't be allowed to continue.

Roche hoped Aggie would understand.

The wet blood started to pool beneath him, sticking to the cross instead of dripping to the floor.

Turning his head, he saw Aggie had her pistol aimed at the Doctor.

Good girl, he thought.

His strength was fading as the blood flowed out of his body.

He willed her to hurry up and shoot.

CHAPTER 52

AGGIE

"Choose quickly," Chapman taunted, "before he's beyond saving..."

The gunshot echoed, and Chapman fell, a hole drilled through his forehead as Aggie rushed to her father's side.

"Just hold my hand," he whispered.

Aggie took his hand as a tear rolled down her cheek.

CHAPTER 53

ROCHE

So this was death, Roche thought.

He managed to smile at Aggie. Having a daughter these last two years had been incredible. She was full of fire, a woman capable of anything he could do, and so much more. Roche wished he had more time to spend with her, but it wasn't going to happen.

Summoning what was left of his strength, he whispered. "I love you, Aggie."

She squeezed his hand. "I love you too, Papa."

Papa. Hearing Aggie call him that somehow made it all worth it. She'd be okay, Aggie would. She was strong, molded by circumstances he hated to think about, but willing to do the hard work to get the job done.

As she looked down at him, tears in her eyes, he focused on her resemblance to Ysidra. He'd loved her more than anything, carried her memory through a brutal war and across the western plains as an Army sergeant.

He wished he could see her again, to tell her how proud he was of their daughter, that she'd done a hell of a job raising her in spite of the circumstances fate and her father dealt them.

His chest hurt, no doubt because his heart was trying to pump blood that wasn't there.

But his girl had finished the job. Ray Spencer and the Doctor were dead.

He could die now.

And he did.

CHAPTER 54

AGGIE

Aggie found a shovel leaning against the side of the Screaming House, and picked a spot under a tall oak tree to dig her father's grave. The sun was high over the mountains when she threw down the last shovelful of dirt. With a final tear, she planted a cross made from two stakes tied together as a makeshift headstone.

"Sorry, Papa."

Five bodies were laid out at the base of the cross. Aggie hoped the vultures had a feast.

Going to the corral, she opened the gate and swung aboard her horse. They'd taken good care of him--even assholes knew the importance of a good horse. That they'd figured on killing her and keeping the horse didn't bother her, she'd have done the same thing if the roles had been reversed.

Leaving the gate open, she rode to the top of the canyon, her horse nimbly stepping around the boulder. The vultures took flight as she approached, circling over the bodies, waiting for a chance to return.

At the top of the cliff, she paused and looked back. She didn't want to leave her father here, alone in a place she'd likely never see again. But she also knew it was a place he'd have loved under different circumstances.

Far beyond the Screaming House, she saw a cloud of dust rising off the plains. Riders, and lots of them.

The Marshal was coming.

Typical, arriving after the mess was cleaned up.

Aggie looked south, across the rangeland to the mountains beyond. Somewhere out there was Ojinaga, a place she'd once called home, but no longer did. But it was home to her only surviving family, and she did have a message to deliver.

Spurring her horse, she continued up the path, the first steps on a long journey.

END

Acknowledgements

This novella would not have been possible without the help of a number of people, to whom I am sincerely thankful.

Carietta and A.R. for serving as ARC Readers and making the story better.
Rebecca for her editing expertise and creative ideas.
Cyan for being Cyan.

Wednesday for her attempts at editing assistance and technical support.
Atlas for the distractions.
Anna for her love and support.

And you, the reader, for picking up this book and reading this far.
Thank you.

D.L. Winchester

D.L. Winchester lives in the foothills of southern Appalachia. A former mortician, his work searches the darkness to find tales worth telling. He is the author of over three hundred obituaries, numerous short stories, and the collections *Shadows of Appalachia* and *A Terrible Place and Other Flashes of Horror*. In his spare time, he can be found searching for inspiration in the world around him and trying to keep his children from becoming the next generation of horror villains.

ALSO BY D.L. WINCHESTER

Shadows of Appalachia

A Terrible Place and Other Flashes of Darkness

Stories To Take To Your Grave #1
(Anthology short story)

Judicial Homicide: Tales of Executions
(Anthology short story)

Undertaker Books

www.undertakerbooks.com

If you are a fan of horror stories and tales,
you'll want to follow Undertaker Books.

We're bringing you stories to take to your grave.

SIGN UP FOR OUR NEWSLETTER ONLINE

Made in the USA
Columbia, SC
07 February 2025